Acknowledgements

I would like to start by thanking my family for supporting me and constantly reading and rereading my story. Next, I would like to thank my work family, Summit Intermediate, you guys have helped me with illustrations, editing, moral support, and guidance. Without any of you I would not have been able to do any of this.

The Adventures of Unknown Heroes

Colton Lee

Published by Colton Lee, 2021.

This is a work of fiction. Similarities to real people, places, or events are entirely coincidental.

THE ADVENTURES OF UNKNOWN HEROES

First edition. May 12, 2021.

Copyright © 2021 Colton Lee.

ISBN: 979-8215516676

Written by Colton Lee.

Table of Content

Chapter 1
Sword Of Power

In the small town of Elberta during a brutal winter, the fight for our way of life begins. Our warriors don't even know they will be chosen, they are just trying not to be chosen to answer questions in math. That's right our heroes are just kids.

Like many kids in her school A.B. was looking for a reason not to go to class. Her and her best friend were split up this year and had different lunches. She tried to get out of class to walk by the cafeteria and say hi to Kay.

While walking down the hall of her school, A.B. found a brick with engravings that she had never seen before.

"When two keep each other as strong as ten,
will they find the strength to begin."

As she read those words she thought of her friend Kay, because they always were stronger together. A.B. ran through the hallway and found Kay sitting down to eat her lunch... pizza, A.B.'s favorite.

"OH pizza... no wait, Kay come here I want to show you something!" A.B. blurted out into the lunchroom. Kay looks at her pizza then looks at A.B. "Grrr," Kay muttered as she ran and dumped her lunch and went over to A.B.

"You know I was really looking forward to that pizza today, right?" Kay said, just a little annoyed.

A.B. took Kay and showed her the brick she found down a little storage hallway, somewhere she really should not be. Today she was skipping class because she hadn't worked on her paper that was due today.

Together they decided to see if they could find more stones around the school. For now, they needed to get back to class, if A.B. skipped math again her teacher was calling her parents...and she really doesn't want them to know she has been skipping class. A.B knew she would get grounded and had big plans with Kay this weekend.

On the way to math the girls walked by a statue of the school mascot. As the girls looked up at this giant tiger holding a sword, like he is going into battle, Kay asked, "Why does a tiger need a sword?"

"Well, you know, a tiger with big claws isn't scary enough, let's give him a big sword too." A.B. laughingly said. "You have to admit it is a pretty awesome sword!"

"We have got to hurry, math is about to start," Kay exclaimed.

At the end of the day A.B. waited for Kay to give her a ride home. Kay came running like someone said there was free ice cream in the parking lot. Kay blurted out, "I have been waiting to talk to you! I went back to the statue while I was "going to the Nurse." I wanted to draw a picture of the sword."

With a glimmer in her eye, A.B. squealed, "OOOhhh I want to see your picture; I love seeing your drawings!"

Annoyed, Kay grunted, "Forget about the picture, I found something on the sword! First, it's called the Sword of Power..."

A.B. chuckles, "Sounds... Powerful."

Getting a little more impatient, Kay declared, "Would you stop, there is more! I found another engraving and it really sounds unnerving."

The two shall stand before the protector of good and face Alioth, the Sky Tiger. Once bested he will surrender his sword to the worthy!

"Ok, so I have a question, actually I have all the questions!" A.B. said in amazement.

"I know! Is it talking about the same two from the other engraving?" asked Kay.

"Who is it talking about? We should ask the Principal, Dr. Quackerman, and see if she knows anything about it."

"Really, Dr. Quackerman?" Kay said sharply.

"Don't worry, Ashley, is a friend of the family, she's kind of like a second mom to me. I stay with her when my parents are out of town. If anyone could help us it would be her!" explained A.B.

The girls drove over to Dr. Quackerman's house. They quickly went to the door and A.B. knocked with a little too much excitement.

"Girls, this is a surprise! Is everything ok? Come on in and I'll grab us all some sweet tea." said Ashley with a little bit of alarm in her voice.

Ashley took the girls into the kitchen and poured everyone a glass of good Ol' southern sweet tea. It really is more like sugar water, but no one was complaining.

"Momma Ash, we found some stuff at the school today and we were wondering if you know anything about it?" A.B. said as she explained everything they found with the engravings.

"Honestly girls, I have never seen anything like that before, and I have cleaned that sword many times. I've worked in this school building for 20 years and I have never seen any bricks with engravings either, but I will look on Monday."

"Well, I hate to interrupt but it is getting late, and I need to get home soon." Kay announced.

Ashley walked the girls to the door and told the girls goodnight. Kay called her parents and asked if she could spend the weekend at A.B.'s house. On their way home they swung by Kay's house and grabbed her stuff. The whole way back to A.B.'s the girls talked about the two riddles they saw at school and tried to figure out what they could mean. It was late when the girls got home and they were both exhausted, so they ate and went to bed early. As the girls begin to fade off into dreamland, a bright light shines in A.B. 's room. There stood a girl not much older than the girls were.

"Please do not be afraid! My name is Remi, and I am the Great Great Granddaughter of Merlin. I am here about the Sword of Power! I come from a time long ago, you might know it as the Dark Ages. There are 5 swords scattered around in your time. I had to get them away from a great evil before he could destroy them. Ragnar and his army will be coming, looking for these swords to destroy them. They are the only things that can stop him, we must find them first. Only the worthy can carry the swords and the price it will cost to be chosen."

"I'm going to regret this, but what is the price?" A.B. moaned.

"A friend closer than family. If you are successful their lives will be spared, but shall you fail they will have no choice but to join Ragnar's army!" replied Remi.

A.B. and Kay looked at each other, as if they were having a conversation, but no one spoke for several minutes.

"I don't think we have much of a choice here Annabeth. It really scares me, but if we don't go through with it the world will be in danger. This is our chance to finally do something that matters, something bigger than us!" Kay confidently exclaimed.

"Yeah, I guess you are right. We will be the unknown heroes that saved the world. No one is ever going to believe that two teenage girls from Elberta fought an ancient evil and saved the world. Let's do it anyway!" A.B. said less confidently.

With a little bit of worry in her voice, Kay muttered, "Honestly, I don't even believe we are going to do this. I can't even imagine trying to tell someone about this. They might put us in a padded room if we tell people."

The girls again look at each other for a few minutes with so much weighing on their minds. On one hand they could just walk away and hope this is all just some prank and all will be ok. On the other hand, they know if they don't do something now than when the world is in trouble it will be all their fault.

"We must go retrieve the sword tonight. I don't want there to be innocent people around to get hurt!" Remi announced with some urgency.

"HURT, what exactly are we getting ready to walk into!" yelled A.B.

"You will have to battle Alioth, the Sky Tiger, also known as your school's mascot. If you truly are the one to wield the Sword of Power then when you begin battling him, you will have all the skills and power transferred from the sword to you and you might have a chance to defeat him. If you are not the chosen one, well let's just hope that doesn't happen." revealed Remi.

"I believe in you Annabeth! You are an amazing person. No one could pick someone more deserving of being the chosen one. You are kind, caring, loyal, and strong; all of which show you can handle all the power without being corrupted." declared Kay.

"Ok...let's go do this before I throw up or pass out!" whimpered A.B.

A.B. drove everyone to the school but she really doesn't remember much of the drive. All she could think about was fighting Tony the Tiger or Alioth or some tiger with wings. When they looked around the school, they found a window cracked open and decided to climb in quietly. A.B. and Kay were used to sneaking in and out of the school for lunch which made this a breeze, but Remi got stuck because she forgot to take off her staff.

"Girls can you give me a hand, I'm stuck!" Remi pleaded.

The girls struggled to get her through but once they could turn her staff and get it through, they all stood in Mr. Zu's math classroom. Kay peeked out the door and spotted the night custodian walking down the hall away from them. He had headphones on and didn't seem to notice any of the noises from their struggle. They quietly snuck down the hallway, past the cafeteria and into the gym. The Tiger statue was in the corner of the gym right under the scoreboard.

"They always bring the statue into the gym for basketball games, it should be over here." commented A.B., "How are we supposed to activate this...battle."

"It should *Activate* once you touch the sword. As soon as you pull the sword from his hands, hopefully you will feel the power flow through you, but be ready even with all that power it won't be easy to defeat Alioth the protector of the sword." warned Remi.

"I... can't...make...it...budge! Maybe if I climb up and stand on top, I can pull the sword up and out of his hands. (A.B. grunts and pulls but still nothing happens) Kay come give me a hand and help me work it loose!" A.B. stated.

A.B. and Kay push each other and try harder. This makes the two as strong as 10 people and allows them to pull the sword from Alioth's hands. A.B. begins to swing the sword around like she has been doing it all her life.

"Wow this sword is so light. I feel the power of the sword. This is awesome!" A.B. squealed.

All at once everyone froze like a deer hearing an acorn fall from a tree. The heavy footsteps of a 7-foot-tall beast, stepping down from his stand got everyone's attention. His face was somewhere between a man and a tiger. The eyes though were all tiger, and they were focused on A.B. He was a massive figure, and he was ready for a fight. He let out a loud roar and charged at A.B, and in a blink of an eye the two met with a sound like thunder crashing. Claws and blades were flying wildly, and it seemed an equal match. Alioth knocked A.B. to the ground and her sword skidded across the floor. Alioth moved in to finish her. In that moment you could feel the air get thick like molasses and no one breathed. Before Alioth got too close he stopped in his tracks as Kay's shoe flew across the gym and struck him in the head. Alioth turned with fire in his eyes and began moving towards Kay. Kay picked up the sword as she stood under the basketball goal waiting, ready for a fight to save her friend. A.B. leaped to her feet and rushed to her friend's side.

"I think we have to fight together! It took both of us to pull the sword, it's going to take both of us to defeat him!" Annabeth said with some fire in her voice.

The girls rushed into action, fighting Alioth, passing the sword back and forth, overwhelming Alioth. As he fell back against the bleachers he said, "Go ahead and finish me, I am no match for the both of you!" A.B. takes the sword and points it at Alioth. He closed his eyes in anticipation, but nothing happened. When he opened his eyes, he saw both girls kneeling against the sword.

"We will not take the life of such an amazing protector. Instead, we would love for you to fight with us. The true enemy is Ragnar, and it will take all of us standing side by side."

"You truly are the chosen ones and are worthy of the Sword of Power. I would be honored to fight next to you." Alioth said as he stood and bowed to the girls.

"Well now that the easy part is finished..." Remi barely spoke before being cut off by A.B.

"Easy part... are you serious! Did you miss us fighting this big fluff ball... no offense! How much harder can it get; I mean we almost died!" A.B. furiously announced.

"Now we must find the other four swords and their bearers. Then we must learn to fight together as one unit, and finally we find Ragnar and his army and hope we are strong enough to defeat them and save our world." Remi said solemnly.

Everyone sat quietly for what seemed forever when A.B. broke the silence and said, "SOOO easy peasy..."

Kay rolled her eyes and laughed a little bit, but the weight of Remi's statement made it hard to enjoy A.B.'s quirkiness.

"Thankfully, one of these swords is not far away in Castleport. The rest though will take some time and travel to find. I am afraid you will not see your families for a while once we start on our journey. Take tonight to spend time with them, hug them and prepare for the possibility you may never see them again." Remi knew what she was asking of the girls, but she also knew what would happen if she didn't ask.

Annabeth was the only one who slept but to be fair she could sleep through a hurricane. I guess battling an Ancient Protector can make you tired. The next morning, they all met at A.B.'s house and loaded up A. B's car. Remi gave A.B. directions to the school where the next sword was hidden. With farm fields all around the school they were truly in the middle of nowhere. Before entering the school Alioth changed forms to look more like a teenage boy.

"Hey A.B., doesn't your dad work here? Do you think he would believe us? Do you think he will get mad and send us home?" probed Kay.

"There is only one way to find out. Let's go see my dad!" A.B. expressed with a little bit of anxiety in her voice.

The group walked in and went to the front desk and spoke to Jan. A.B. has talked to her many times when she would come with her dad to work and has learned that Mrs. Jan is a very sassy and sometimes blunt woman, but she is also extremely sweet and kind once you get to know her. While A.B. talked to Jan about finding her dad, Kay spotted Mr. Lee heading down the hallway.

"Hey Ya'll, is everything ok? Did something happen? I don't see any police so either you outran them, or you are not in trouble..." joked Mr. Lee.

"Dad, first off, it's not funny, secondly we really need your help, can we go somewhere and talk?" said A.B.

"This is beginning to sound like maybe you outran the police; am I now an accessory to your crimes..." Colt continued to joke.

A.B. getting a little more annoyed "Dad seriously we need to tell you something!"

They all step into the empty art room and the girls begin to tell A.B. 's dad everything that has happened, but the more they told him the more puzzled he began to look.

"I don't know if this is some elaborate joke or what but like I told the girls from my class, I just don't believe it. I couldn't see any engravings and I really find it hard to believe y'all battle some giant tiger man..." Colt stopped speaking as Alioth changed back into his Tiger form. "I must be losing my mind, my students finally got to me!"

"Dad, meet Alioth... you know the giant tiger man we battled. Don't worry he is on our side now; he was just protecting the sword before." Said Annabeth.

In his best impression of McConaughey, "Alright, Alright, Alright, let's say I do believe you. Is there anything I can say or do that will stop you from trying to save the world? And as I ask it, I know my answer, you girls don't back down from a challenge. I'm guessing you won't be home for dinner tonight, huh?" Colt knew he wouldn't see Annabeth for a while. "I had two of my students come in earlier telling me a story kind of like yours. I thought they were crazy and told them to go play. I think we need to go find them and let y'all talk. Just remember they are only 5th graders, try not to scare them too much."

Chapter 2
Sword of Sight

Eliza and Emma had been best friends from birth. Their parents met at the hospital when the girls were born. Eliza, although small, has a very demanding presence. On the other hand, Emma is softer spoken and observes what is going on around her.

A few days before Christmas break, Eliza and Emma decide to huddle by the wall while at recess trying but failing to stay warm. Emma, being the observant one, noticed a brick buried down at the bottom corner of the wall, behind some rocks, that looked like it had some writing engraved on it. They quickly dug away the rocks to see what the brick said.

When two step back and wait, they can use their hearts to change fate."

A little confused, Emma asked, "What in the world does it mean, and why is it just buried here?"

"I have no clue, but you know who has been here for like ever and might know! Mr. Lee!" exclaimed Eliza.

When another student asked to go to the nurse, the girls decided to sneak in behind her. They go running around the halls looking for Mr. Lee.

While running a little ahead of Emma, Eliza yells, "Let's go down the East hallway, he hangs out in the art room when he doesn't have class!"

The girls looked in the art room, the music room, and the library, but came up empty. Just when they were giving up on finding him, Mr. Lee walked out of the Office.

"Mr. Lee, Mr. Lee, Mr. Lee! We need you to follow us, we need to show you something and see if you know anything about it." Eliza said impatiently.

Mr. Lee followed the girls outside and down the side of the building. Eliza pointed to the bottom corner brick and asked him if he knew what the phrase meant.

"Girls, I don't see any words. If you are messing with me again, then you got me, and I am freezing. Now go play and I'm going in to get warm." Mr. Lee said over the chattering of his teeth.

As Mr. Lee was heading back inside, he got a call over his radio to come to the office, his daughter was here to see him.

Completely confused, Emma asked, "Why couldn't he see it? Its giant letters written in brick, kind of hard to miss!"

A few minutes later Mr. Lee, followed by his daughter and friends, came running out of the building looking for Eliza and Emma.

"Girls, there you are. Can you please come inside to my room; we need to talk to you about the brick?" Mr. Lee said with some urgency.

They all headed inside and found Mr. Lee's classroom. Mr. Lee pulled the door closed and had A.B. close all the blinds.

"Ladies, this is my daughter Annabeth and her friends. They have found some similar bricks at their school and know a little about them. They want to talk to you." explained Mr. Lee.

A.B. started the conversation, "Ok, this is going to be a lot to take in and it's going to sound crazy..."

Kay added, "First off, you will be the only two people that can see the words on the bricks. Only those who are worthy of being the chosen can see it."

Eliza quickly interrupted her, "Wait chosen... chosen for what?"

In her most ominous voice A.B. said, "Well... to save the world!"

Kay jumped in, "I thought we weren't supposed to freak them out, remember!"

A.B. corrected her previous statement, "To be preventers of some mildly bad situations that may or may not end life as we know it... better?"

Quickly Eliza responded, "NO not really, but we are in... what do we need to do?"

Emma seemed like she was going to jump out of her chair with excitement. She looked around at everyone and then finally blurted out, "Do we get like superpowers... can I fly or go invisible or something!"

Remi looked at Emma a little puzzled and said, "No, no powers like that, but you do get a really cool sword that gives you the power of sight. It is being protected by an Ancient Protector that looks like a giant eagle. It will most likely be a statue of your school mascot holding a sword."

Eliza thought for a minute, "... I don't remember seeing an eagle statue around the school. I know years ago my dad said they took it down because someone didn't like our mascot having a sword."

Mr. Lee began talking, partly to himself but everyone was listening. "Last I knew they put it down in the basement, but last year they sealed off the entrance to the basement. I heard there was a sinkhole in the floor, and they decided it wasn't safe to enter anymore. I have heard rumors that there might be another way in, but it could just be stories of bored custodians."

They decided they had to try. Everyone followed Colt into the custodian room. As he looked around, he found a bookcase and noticed a breeze coming from behind it. As they moved the bookcase, they uncovered a hole broken into the wall with a tunnel that led off into darkness. As they slowly felt their way down the tunnel they came to an opening. The room was dimly lit and was clearly not part of the school. The walls were massive and made of natural stone. It was an underground cave, there were many of these around this part of the country. The group noticed a big worn door on the other side of the cave. As they approached the door, they realized just how big this door really was. Alioth turned into his 7-foot-tall Protector form and still struggled to pull it open. Again, another long hallway. This hallway went from natural limestone walls to more modern steel plated walls with lights every so often. Finally, they came to a door that said basement exit. This must have been an emergency exit, for just in case someone got locked in. I guess they forgot about it when sealing off the basement. Colt warned everyone, "Remember, they sealed off the basement because the floor is unstable, be careful where you step."

With an eerie creek, they opened the door to a dark and stale smelling room. The air rushed out of the room like it was waiting to escape some unknown beast waiting in the darkness. It sent chills down Emma's neck. Remi used what little magic she could still do to make a glowing orb that was bright enough to show most of the enormous room in front of them. Everyone went in different directions making careful and deliberate moves, as to avoid openings in the floor.

Eliza was the first to shout, "I found Big Bird and he has a sword!"

Emma was the first one to make it over to her and she added, "Well he looks a little tougher than Big Bird... and his eyes... They are like looking into my soul. They look like balls of fire from the depths of a volcano."

"Ok guys, so do we just take the sword and get out of here?" asked Eliza.

"Does it say anything on the sword or somewhere around the sword?" A.B. questioned.

Emma looked closely, "I see something... can you shine your magic light bulb over here."

When two with one heart see, they decide the way it should be.

Kay looked at A.B., "I think we should tell them what happens next..."

"I knew it couldn't be as easy as just taking the sword. What do we have to do... do we have to eat something weird or do some weird tasks?" probed Eliza.

The girls looked at each other then began to tell them that once they pulled the sword, they would have to fight a giant eagle ancient protector.

"So, we need to work together to kick Big Bird's tail feathers?" Eliza laughed nervously.

"His name is Aetos Dios, not Big Bird. He is known as the messenger of Zeus himself. He has been trained personally by all the Greek gods. Do not mock or underestimate him." warned Remi.

Eliza and Emma took a deep breath and approached Aetos Dios and reached out towards the sword. As the girls embraced the sword and felt its power, they began to see their battle play out in many ways, but only one showed them how to beat Aetos Dios. The girls immediately went into their battle positions and knew exactly what they needed to do. As Aetos stepped down, they sprang into action. They knew every step to avoid and exactly when to dodge his attacks. Finally, Emma saw her opening, she jumped up from behind Aetos and struck him with the butt of the sword. Aetos stumbled and fell to his knees.

"I see I am finished, and you have out matched me. I surrender and ask for your mercy." Aetos announced in defeat.

Eliza looked around at everyone and then back at Aetos, "Stand great protector. We need you to stand and fight with us."

Unfortunately, after such a battle more of the floor had caved in. The group had to take turns crossing a narrow piece of floor to get back to the door. One by one they walked across, everyone made it ok until Eliza started across. The narrow piece of floor began to crumble under her feet, and she had to act fast. Her power of sight kicked in and she could see exactly what move she needed to do next. First, she jumped to a nearby ledge barely big enough to hold her, but it held firm. Now she grabbed on to a cord hanging from the roof and swung across to a small piece of floor close to the door but missed her footing and fell. Aetos managed to fly over and reach out and grab her hand just before she fell. It was clear now that he was on their side. They all made it back to the school and went back to Mr. Lee's classroom.

The four girls huddled up and clearly were having a heated discussion. They would look up every now and then and then go right back to the huddle. After about 15 minutes they finally join everyone else at the tables up front.

A.B. began, "Dad, we have been talking and because of your knowledge of historical stuff and well it will make it easier for us to travel having an adult with us, we would like to ask you to come with us."

Emma added, "Plus we would all feel better having someone looking out for us like you always do."

"You will have to keep your corny jokes to a minimum though!" Eliza quickly threw out there.

Mr. Lee pulled out one of his many maps and laid it across the table. Remi began to mark off the places where the last three swords would be found. She began telling them what swords were left as they looked at the various locations. Now the group had to decide which sword to go after next, the Sword of Speed, the Sword of Fire, or the Sword of Chaos. They all agreed to hold off on the Sword of Chaos; it just sounded intimidating. After some debate they decided to go after the Sword of Speed next. It looked like they were headed to Coeval, three days of traveling ahead of them more depending on this snowstorm moving in. They loaded up Mr. Lee's truck and hooked up his 5th wheel and headed out across the country.

As the group got close to Coeval the snow began to come down so hard it was like a scene from Star Wars when they jumped into lightspeed. They pulled over in a nearby parking lot to let the storm pass. Once the storm began to let up, they realized they were in the parking lot of Coeval High School. Due to the storm hitting so fast, some students had already made it to the school before they canceled. Everyone was trying to figure out how they would get home on these icy roads.

Chapter 3
Sword Of Speed

Klaus arrived early to school for cross country practice. He knew it would be crazy to be out running in this weather, but he needed to get faster to beat A.J. at the next meet. Klaus and A.J. have been rivals for as long as they can remember. Like many rivalries this one started over a girl. Both boys have been showing off for June ever since they were in first grade. She never really paid either much attention, but it never stopped them from trying. While Klaus was changing in the locker room, he noticed a brick behind the edge of the lockers. He couldn't see enough to read, so he tried to push the lockers away just enough to read it. As he struggled for several minutes, A.J. walked in and looked bewildered at Klaus.

"Is this some weird workout that you think is going to make you better than me?" A.J. said sarcastically.

"No, I don't need anything to make me better than you, I was born that way!" exploded Klaus. "If you must know I found some writing on the wall over here and I'm trying to figure out what it says."

"It would help if you knew how to read, do you want me to sound it out for you?" jabbed A.J.

"It is hidden behind these lockers, can you just shut your pie hole for a second and help me move them?" pleaded Klaus.

The two boys worked together to move the lockers. They struggled for a few minutes but managed to move them enough to see the whole brick.

When two worlds collide, they shall learn to move as fluid as the tide.

Klaus thought to himself, "Talking about two worlds colliding, A.J.'s parents are big donors to the school, and he can choose whatever team he wants to be on. Meanwhile I come from nothing, and I have been fighting tooth and nail to get on this team and earn my spot."

A.J., talking a little softer, "Any idea what this is? I mean why would this be in our locker room and hidden behind the lockers?"

"Well, Coach was here when they remodeled the locker room, I'm sure he saw it when they repainted it. Maybe he looked into it already." answered Klaus.

The boys decided to work together, at least for the moment. They both were very curious about the engraving, plus they can go back to hating each other tomorrow.

They head to the coach's office and find Coach Evan on the phone, trying to help get students home since school got canceled too late. It seems Coach was one of the few teachers that made it before getting the message.

After he got off the phone, the boys asked Coach Evan about the engraving. When Coach didn't know what they were talking about they took Coach into the locker room to show him.

" Fellas, I don't know what you're getting at but if you don't get my lockers back where they go in the next two minutes, you will be owing me an extra hour of workout time. Then again maybe I'm working you too hard, I've got you seeing words that aren't there...how about you boys take this morning off. Do you guys have a way to get home?"

A.J. quickly answered, "I have my Corvette out front!" just to rub it in Klaus's face.

It backfired on A.J. when Coach asked him to give Klaus a ride home. The boys get changed and head out to the parking lot arguing the whole time about what the stone might mean. They were so engrossed in their argument they didn't even notice the group standing by the truck a few parking spots away.

Mr. Lee approached the boys and asked, "Hey, sorry to bother you, but we overheard you talking about some writing on the wall. We actually have similar moments; do you mind talking with us all for a minute?"

They all went inside the camper and sat to talk. A.B. told about her experience first and then Eliza talked about hers next. Both Alioth and Aetos changed into their protector forms to help convince the boys.

"Wait, so we get to use a sword, fight bad guys, and hang out with some pretty awesome girls... where do I sign up!?" exclaimed A.J. with a little too much eagerness.

"Wow, classy as usual, but I will help too. I always wanted to join the army and fight for my country. This sounds about on par for that." stated Klaus as he looked at Kay then looked away quickly.

Kay blushed and quickly looked at Annabeth, who smiled and made kissy faces at her. Kay's face went from pink to red as she pushed A.B. away before anyone could see.

Remi began telling everyone, "The sword of speed will not be an easy one to bear. The goddess Nefere is quick and fierce. She will not hesitate to do what she needs to protect the Sword of Speed."

As the others talked about their swords coming from a statue of their school mascots, the boys began to fear theirs might too. The only statue they can think of is out by the track and football field. It must stand 10 feet tall with the body of a horse and the torso of a beautiful lady holding a giant sword with a blade that looks almost Persian with its curves. The sword itself looked to be 3 feet long, it was more proportioned to the woman than to the mustang. Regardless she looked like she was ready to stampede and battle.

"How exactly do we get up there and get the sword and then get down before she bucks us off?" asked A.J.

Klaus was already climbing up the statue. All he could figure is grab it, jump, and try to roll down the hill with as little hurting as possible. A.J. immediately ran up and started climbing too not to be out done by Klaus. They both made it to the top and reached the sword at the same time, releasing it from Nefere's grip. Moving quickly caused them both to lose their footing and they fell off the side of the statue. Somehow, they both began to move quickly enough to run down the side and across the football field in a blink of an eye.

Confused Klaus exclaimed, "What just happened? How did we go from there to here?"

Before anyone could even process what happened, Nefere ran down and kicked both boys 5 yards back. They laid there looking at each other trying to figure out what kind of a truck just hit them. Nefere moved like lightning, she would be attacking before anyone saw her move. The boys were flying all over the place and they were looking to be in bad shape. Neither of them would help the other, they tried to attack on their own but could never land a single attack. The boys finally regroup and decide they need to work together again. As they begin to attack, one moves in from the front, while the other comes in from the side. "Crack." They landed their first hit. And then another. Finally, they were getting into a groove and Nefere could not keep up with both boys. She finally collapsed on the 50-yard line. She tried to stand but her front legs wobbled, and she fell again.

Weakly, Nefere admitted, "You are too quick even for me. I am no match for you. The sword belongs to you if you work together. It only works when you put your differences aside and work as one. I would be honored if you would allow me to join you on your journey."

As the group gathered by the flagpole, they knew things were only going to get tougher and even more dangerous from here. Mr. Lee and A.B. held hands and began to pray, slowly everyone else joined in as they circled the flag. Mr. Lee started the prayer, and everyone took turns praying to help get them through what was coming their way. They knew it was going to take more than these swords to save everyone.

Mr. Lee pulled out his map of Renanne Providence and the group decided to head towards the Sword of Fire next. These last two swords will prove to be the most dangerous to take possession of. Remi informed everyone the Sword of Fire would be protected by a Dragon and the Sword of Chaos would be protected by the goddess of chaos Eris. Remi is still trying to figure out how to get Eris on their side once she is defeated... if she is defeated.

Mr. Lee mapped out their route and decided going through the Canton Mountains would be the quickest way to get to Odsdale, the home of the next sword. It might be the quickest, but it would not be easy. The Canton Mountains are known to be very perilous to those not familiar with navigating through them. There are creatures many talk about seeing when passing through, but most think they are just a legend. One way or another they were about to find out what lies ahead.

Chapter 4
Canton Mountains

After days of traveling the caravan grew close to the base of the Canton Mountains. They knew this would not be an easy trek, but they were going to try to get through as quickly and safe as possible. Colt felt responsible for everyone with him, and he knew even though they were going into battle at some point, they were still just kids. He knew Annabeth and Kay both were saved because he had been there for both and led them to Christ, but he prayed for the rest for now. He knew at some point along the way he would need to try to show Christ to the others. If anything goes wrong, he will never forgive himself for not at least trying.

There were two paths before them. One went through the mountain and seemed to be straight through, and the other went up and over but seemed to be very windy. As the group approached the beginning of both roads, they saw warning signs.

In lies a beast that moves in the shadows. His touch burns and his breath can kill. Only those that are worthy can face him and live.

Going over will surely put any that are worthy in the ground. Those that travel with them are the only ones who will be spared.

They argued for a while but finally decided the only choice they had would be to split up and meet back on the other side. Those that were chosen went together into the tunnel and faded into the darkness. Colt, Remi, and the three protectors all set out across the mountain in hopes to meet the others on the other side. As A.B. and the others descended into the mountain it got darker and darker, they could tell someone was watching them but could never quite see anyone. Sometimes in the corner of their eyes they would see some movement but just as quick as they would see it, it would be gone. This route was proving to be a lot longer and more rugged than they expected. It was getting late, so they found an area that tucked back into the wall giving them three walls of protection and they set up camp for the night. A.J. and Klaus volunteered to take first watch and let the girls get some sleep.

"You know it's kind of funny how life can throw you a curve ball sometimes. I mean we have been enemies for as long as I can remember but now, we must rely on each other to fight. Honestly, I'm tired of fighting with you anyways. We used to be friends until a girl came between us. I don't even think she cares for either of us anyways. Can we start over and do this right, fight together not against each other?" Klaus said as he stared into the fire.

"Man, I know what you mean. I felt like we had to fight because everyone expected it after a while. I think we can be unstoppable as friends. I mean we did kick that giant horse's butt right?" laughed A.J.

Meanwhile, back up on the mountain, Colt was taking the group through very rough, slippery, and dangerous terrain. The roads were iced over and winding all over the place with steep drop offs. Colt felt like someone was watching them from the ridges above, but he never could spot anyone. It would be tough though to see anyone in all this snow, so he just continued pushing forward looking for a place to set up camp for the night.

Up ahead they saw a cave just big enough to pull the truck into and to camp inside. Colt and Alioth built a fire and took the first watch. The air outside the cave was whipping by like a freight train, making a howling sound that sent shivers down Colt's spine. It made it hard to see anything outside the cave with the snow blowing around making a wall of white shielding anything on the outside from being seen. Colt couldn't shake the feeling again that someone or something was watching them again, but there was no way he could see anything out there.

Back inside the mountain the boys were just waking up the girls to switch shifts and try to get a few hours of sleep. Just as they were laying down, they heard someone scream. They jumped up just in time to see A.B. and Kay fighting, but they couldn't see who they were fighting. Every time they would strike it though, you could see a fiery glow where they hit.

Klaus quickly shouted at A.J., "It glows when we hit it, if we hit it quickly, we can see more of him. Let's work together and strike it rapidly!"

The boys rush the beast and land not one, not two, not three, not even four, but fifteen hits: lighting the beast up like a firework show. Now they could see who they were fighting; they all grabbed their swords and formed a circle around the beast, taking turns attacking him until it ran away. They decided it was time to pack up and keep moving to get out of this mountain before the beast came back with friends.

Meanwhile on top of the mountain, the Protectors have been woken up because a giant figure was approaching the entrance to the cave. Colt was not going to wait and see what it was before waking them, this creature looked to be at least 8 feet tall and seemed to have a tail that was swishing back and forth. Alioth, Neferes, Aetos, and Remi stood on either side of the opening of the cave wall while Colt stood in the opening for the beast to be focused on. As it got closer Colt noticed it also had wings and walked more like a horse. As it finally walked into the opening Colt realized he was looking at a real live Griffin. He had only heard stories before about them, but everyone thought they were extinct now. The stories say Griffins are extremely aggressive and destructive creatures unless they find someone they want as a rider. The problem is they are very picky which is why they were thought to be extinct. Colt froze, he thought to himself that he would die right here and never get to see A.B. again. The griffin moved closer and let out a blood curdling screech, but then lowered its head and moved slowly towards Colt and began walking around him. It smelled him and nudged him, it even licked him, which was extremely disgusting, but Colt was not going to move or say a thing. Finally, after the longest ten minutes of Colt's life the griffin came face to face with Colt and stared into his eyes and then gently kneeled before him. From everything Colt had read this meant he was to be the Griffin's new rider. As he began to move towards the griffin, so did the other which frightened him. He began to attack the others, wounding Remi and knocking Alioth against the truck. He seemed ok with Aetos and Neferes because of their similarities. Before the griffin could attack Remi again, Colt stepped forward and raised his hands which stopped him in his tracks. The griffin responded to Colt's commands. He truly was the griffin's rider.

"I think I will call you Ranger since you're fierce like an Airborne Ranger." Colt said as everyone watched with amazement.

They gathered their things and got in the truck; Colt told Ranger to follow them down the mountain. As they drove down the trail Colt could see Ranger flying behind them, watching closely making sure not to lose them.

Both groups reached the other side of the mountains and regrouped. After a quick standoff with Ranger and the Chosen, Colt calmed Ranger down and filled the others in on what was going on.

"I can't even get a dog Dad, but you get to have a Griffin, seriously come on!" said A.B. oozing sarcasm.

They gathered around the hood of Colt's truck and looked at the map, they weren't far from Odsdale now. Next stop would be to find the Sword of Fire which meant finding a big mean dragon also. I guess having a Griffin to help with the fight might come in handy since they both can fly, it's the fire part that has everyone worried.

They drove for a few hours and finally saw a sign for Odsdale, Remi then directed them to the Odsdale High School. As they pulled into the parking lot it wasn't hard to see where the next sword would be. On top of the school sat a giant dragon that looked like it was wrapped around the school and at the base of the dragon, right next to his tail was a sword stuck in a rock. It reminded Colt of a story of Merlin and the Sword in the Stone, and he could tell Remi was thinking the same thing.

Chapter 5
Sword Of Fire

It was the first day back to school from Christmas break and Dallas was running late, as usual. His brother Kane was waiting in his Firebird, revving the engine impatiently.

The brothers fought constantly but the moment someone crossed either, they both tag teamed them and never lost a fight. Dallas was 6'7" tall with bright red hair and the temper to go with it, while Kane is only an inch shorter and has much darker red hair. Everyone knows you don't cross the Ember brothers, but they also know they will stand and fight for those in need. The only thing they can't stand more than each other is someone being bullied or treated wrong.

When the boys finally made it to school an hour late, Kane came into the parking lot at full speed leaving tire marks as he did a doughnut around the truck and trailer parked in the back of the parking lot. Kane came to a quick stop, slamming Dallas's head into the dash. The boys ran to the door, but they were locked already. Dallas pushed the speaker button and asked the office if someone could come let them in. while the boys waited outside Dallas was messing around with the sword.

"Look at me I'm the dragon slayer, no one can stop me..." Dallas was interrupted by the school Principal, "Late again, Mr. Ember and again please leave our sword alone. One of these days you're going to break it and somehow hurt yourself and somehow it's going to be my fault, so please just don't!"

Before he stepped away Kane stood beside him, smarting off to the principal as usual. Colt and his crew were watching from the parking lot and noticed the sword began to smoke a little.

"I think we might have found our next two chosen ones, but they are going to be rough!" said Colt, "Let's wait and talk to them after school, maybe take some time to rest while we wait."

It wasn't even lunch time, and the boys were being escorted out the front door and clearly being sent home for the day. Colt figured it was now or never and they approached the boys cautiously.

"Hey guys, we would like to talk to you..." Colt began to say but the boys went into fight mode seeing a large group of people coming at them. After a few minutes of fighting everyone, Alioth and Aetos changed into their protector forms and detained the boys to give Colt a chance to speak to them.

"Guys, we are not here to fight you. We need your help but if you guys are going to be loose cannons, we will save the world without you. "Colt said straight to their faces.

Kane quickly replied' "Save the world, wait a minute I want in. I can control myself; I can't talk for my brother though!"

"I am more in control of myself than my brother ever will be. You can count on us to help anyone. What do you need from us?" asked Dallas.

"Well, you know that sword over there that you got in trouble for messing with. I need you both to go over there and pull it out of the stone, but when you do it is going to wake up that dragon. That dragon is the protector of the sword, and it is going to be mad, and it is going to come after you and us and anyone to get that sword back. We will have to find a way to fight and win against it. So far, all the protectors have surrendered and joined our team and I hope we can do the same here. I am hoping there is some power in the sword that allows you to control the dragon once defeated." stated Colt.

The boys knew the principal would still be watching and waiting for them to drive off, so they would have to be sneaky. They walked through the cars and around the side of the building and walked along the edge of the building just out of the view of the front door. They reached out and grabbed the sword which ignited destroying the rock it was embedded in. The Ember brothers ran to the others, who were already in fighting positions. As the boys took up their positions, they looked at the school and saw... nothing. The dragon wasn't there. Suddenly a shadow moved across them, and they looked to the sky where they could see the dragon flying around in the sky. It circled around and then as quickly as it took to the sky, it began to dive, right towards the group. Dallas noticed the dragon's belly began to glow and yelled at everyone to get out of the way just in time for the dragon to breathe fire where the group had just been standing. Dallas stood and took his sword and began swinging his sword towards the dragon but knew he would never be able to hit it in the air. While he was swinging the sword, Kane noticed the fire on the ground began to dance in a rhythm following the motion of the sword.

Kane shouted at Dallas, "The sword can control the fire, use the fire as a weapon against the dragon!"

The next time the dragon flew low enough, Dallas took the sword and in a deliberate way moved the sword to make the fire move like a fire whip, striking the dragon across the wing. The dragon took a hard plunge into the parking lot landing on a few of the cars. While the dragon was down Dallas passed the sword to Kane who used the sword to make fire chains to hold the dragon down to the ground. They slowly began to approach the dragon and as they got close, they noticed he was about to spit fire right at them. Before they could think, Kane struck the sword down inches from the dragon's snout, allowing the boys to divide the fire, hide behind the sword, and stay safe. Finally, the dragon spoke, "You truly born of fire, meant to be one with and control the sword and fire within. The sword and I are one and I must go with it. I am Thraxal and I am at your service from now on."

The convoy now consisted of Colt's truck and trailer, A.J.'s Corvette, Kane's Firebird, Ranger the Griffin, and Thraxal the Dragon, it was a sight to see coming down the road. Even with everyone together the last sword would be the most difficult. Eris was not going to just give it up and she is known for being an expert in chaos, there is no way to be ready for what she might bring. Everyone would have to be at their best and ready for anything. As the group headed south to Scarbury, they knew it was getting close to time to go after Ragnar and none of the battles so far would compare to the one to come. Everyone traveled in silence, Colt on Ranger, A.B. drove the truck, A.J. followed in his car, Kane followed closely behind in his Firebird, and Dallas flew above on Thraxal. It would be the longest part of their journey so far; it would take them 2 weeks to get to Scarbury. After eight days of traveling through the wide-open fields of lower Renanne, they came to a beautiful lake that looked like it went on for miles. As they pulled in, they saw a sign "Bragg Lake." There was a small town right on the lake and the group went into town to reload on supplies for the rest of their journey. Colt was talking with the town Sheriff about heading down to Scarbury and asked him for the best route. The Sheriff looked at Colt sideways and questioned him why anyone in their right mind would want to go there. After a few minutes of arguing why he should just stay and enjoy Bragg Lake, the Sheriff finally gave him directions down the Bluff River.

As the team loaded supplies and headed out down the trail, they could tell it would not be an easy route. There were no roads from here on, they decided to leave the trailer behind in Bragg City with the Sheriff. The trail went right along the side of Bluff River and when they were at river level, the trail would be washed out and they would have to use Colt's 4-wheel drive to pull out the other cars, making the trip take forever. When they weren't at river level, they drove carefully across ridges that were barely wide enough to drive across and a few times the edges gave way almost causing the team to go plummeting to the river below.

As the group passed through the Rockwall Mountain Range Colt noticed a clearing at the base of the mountains close to the river. The clearing had mountain ridges circling it on all sides with a small opening on the riverside. He thought to himself this would be a good place to come back with everyone to train and set up camp before we march off to war.

After three weeks of traveling and almost losing a few team members, they finally made it to the outskirts of Scarbury. Scarbury seemed like a ghost town. It was clear why the Sheriff was concerned about the group coming here. It looked like a hurricane had swept in from the Baldwin Sea and left few survivors, but the weird thing was hurricanes never came from the Baldwin Sea and it only hit this town and nowhere else.

Chapter 6
Sword Of Chaos

In the wake of the freak Hurricane that suddenly appeared and destroyed most of the town of Scarbury, Emmalyn was searching for other survivors. It was like the hurricane was summoned to Scarbury, it came and just stayed, then disappeared unlike any hurricane she had ever seen or heard of. Emmalyn and a few other students had been just out of town when the hurricane hit. They were working on an art mural on a rock formation a few miles outside of the city limits. Their art teacher talked the mayor into allowing them to capture Scarbury into a mural to bring a little color and beauty back to their town.

Emmalyn ran into Lyndsey sitting on the curb crying outside what used to be her house.

"Hey Lyndsey, have you found any sign of your family?" Emmalyn asked softly.

"No, it's like they just disappeared with the hurricane! I don't know how there is no sign of them anywhere. I don't know if they are alive or ..." Lyndsey was cut off before she could finish her sentence.

"Let's not think like that yet, we don't know anything about what happened here. They got to safety, and they just haven't come back yet. My family is missing too, so for now let's stick together. Mrs. Fin has opened the art room for us to stay in for now, so let's head down there and regroup." Emmalyn said.

As the girls got close to the high school, they noticed it looked untouched, like the hurricane missed it somehow. The high school sat at the center of town and everything around it showed some level of damage, but nothing, not even the trees seemed to be bothered.

Before the girls could think about the implications, they saw a very strange group coming down Main St. It was the Griffin and Dragon flying that really got their attention, neither had seen one in real life. They had drawn pictures and been obsessed with them, but never imagined they would get to see one. It seemed they were coming straight for the school and fast, the girls hid behind the display of the school sword their art teacher made.

"We have to hurry and find someone and see what happened here!" Colt said to the others.

Emmalyn noticed the art teacher Watching from her window, but she looked different. She seemed worried as these newcomers moved closer to the school. In fact, the closer they got the angrier she seemed to get, and just as they reached the parking lot, the sword vanished from above the girls. As quickly as it vanished, it reappeared in Mrs. Fin's hand, in the parking lot, right in front of the others.

Emmalyn couldn't believe what was happening and was still trying to process what happened. She felt like this group wasn't bad and somehow, she was meant to be with them, but she also knew her teacher well and had grown close to her over the last few months. She looked at Lyndsey and then went out and stood between Mrs. Fin and the others. She didn't know what was about to happen or what she could do but she had to try. Mrs. Fin didn't even look at her though, she was set on one girl from the other group that had locked eyes with her. They clearly knew each other and had a past, but there had already been enough devastation here and Emmalyn didn't want to see anymore. As she looked at both, she noticed that her teacher had a look of hatred and anger, but the other girl looked downhearted and sorrowful, like the weight of the world rested on her shoulders. Emmalyn began to understand that her teacher might not be who she thinks she is, and this sword she holds looks much like the swords many of the others carry.

Emmalyn slowly moved out of the way, met with Lyndsey, and told her what she was planning to do... take the sword.

After Lyndsey gave Emmalyn every excuse why they couldn't do this and every reason they would fail, the girls split up and began to move in on the teacher while she was focused on the others.

"Remi, after all this time you have finally come to visit me. You banished me here to guard your sword and wouldn't even let me play with it. Well, I have been regaining my magic and I finally have enough to control your sword and use it against you!" Eris erupted as she changed from her form as Mrs. Fin to her goddess form.

"Eris, we were friends, you were good once, what did I miss? Where did I fail you, my friend? I never wanted this; I still want my best friend back! I sent you here to protect you, to hopefully separate you from the bad magic and let you heal!" cried Remi.

When Eris and Remi became friends centuries ago, neither one had magic yet, but soon they would be of age to start practicing. They became best friends fast and were never seen apart. Once they both got their magic and began learning how to use it, they began to have different ideas about how and when they should use their magic. It began to drive a wedge between the two girls, Remi only liked to use her magic when necessary and only for good intentions, but Eris would use magic whenever she wanted to, and she would use it to get whatever she wanted.

As they got older, Eris became increasingly selfish, and she didn't care who she hurt in the process. Many began to call her evil and feared her, but Remi tried to still hold on to her friend, until one day, Eris used her magic and, in the process, caused a family to get extremely sick and almost die.

Remi knew she couldn't allow her to continue and if she could get her away from her magic, just maybe, she could finally get her friend back.

When Remi had to find protectors to guard the swords, she knew she would have to send Eris without her magic and use a spell on her to do as Remi wanted her to do. Remi hated doing it this way, but she had to do it quickly and couldn't think of another way.

Now staring at Eris and seeing the hatred in her eyes and the chaos she has created; Remi knew it was the wrong choice. She knew now she would have to fight her friend for the sword, and she knew it would be a battle like no other battle the group had fought before. She would have to get everyone ready and hopefully keep everyone alive, including her friend.

Remi noticed the two girls moving in on Eris and realized they were going to try to take the sword. She knew she had to keep her distracted, so she stepped forward and asked Eris, "How have you liked your little vacation here? I see you became an Art Teacher!" She knew it would make her mad and keep her rage focused on Remi.

Emmalyn knew this was her chance and she lunged forward, grabbing the sword from Eris, which caused a horrible storm to] start raging around the team, followed by a freak snowstorm, followed by hail, followed by 70 mph winds and then sunshine. Everyone looked around in shock until Remi spoke up, "The Sword of Chaos can control the weather, I guess when Eris and the other girl touched the sword at the same time, it was confused who to listen to and lost control."

Emmalyn and Lyndsey joined the group and introduced themselves. They knew now they would have to join them against Eris to save what was left of their town and even bring back those they lost.

Eris didn't wait around for everyone to get to know each other, she began the attack first. Her magic had grown immensely powerful, and Remi was having a challenging time fighting a fair fight. The others tried to help but they were no match for her magic. Eliza and Emma used their Sword of Sight and laid out a battle plan for the group. They would have to follow it perfectly to win. It was the only way they saw that ended with them winning. First, Emmalyn and Lyndsey used their sword to cause a downpour creating a wall of rain between the two sides. Next, the Ember brothers would use the Sword of Fire to start up enough fire to create a fire tornado to enclose Eris inside. While Eris is trapped inside the Sword of Speed will be used to keep Remi on the move and where Eris cannot attack her. Finally, amongst all the chaos, A.B will begin the attack with the Sword of Power, followed by Emmalyn and the Sword of Chaos, then all together everything will stop, and the Sword of Speed and Sword of Fire will attack followed by the final blow from Remi. Even with everyone attacking with perfect precision the outcome continues to change in their vision. Eris's will and Remi's compassion continue to make the outcome dance back and forth and it seems it will be a 50/50 shot for the team to win.

This is their only chance, so the team moves into place and begins the attack. First, they distract her with the rain allowing Remi and the boys to use the Sword of Speed to get on the move. As the Ember brothers spread fire in a circle around Eris, they began spinning it creating a fire tornado which sucked all the air out of the center, causing Eris to not be able to use her magic. Slowly Eris began to lose consciousness, this was the window for A.B. to begin her attack. A.B. used her Sword of Power and summoned all the power of the Sky Tiger as she struck Eris, causing the ground around her to split from the force. Emmalyn followed up and used all the force of a hurricane and struck Eris across the parking lot and against the school, shattering all the windows and doors. Dallas came in next, his sword looked more like a fire whip. With a flick and a crack, he used it just like a whip and cracked it right on Remi, causing an explosion at the school. You could just barely see Eris inside the fire slowly start to stand, but before she could get up Remi came in with the boys and in a unified attack the struck sword and magic, causing Eris to collapse. The magic that Remi hit her with took all her magic away again just in time for the final blow from the Sword of Speed to hit, and in her human form, her body could not withstand the attack.

While everybody cheered and celebrated, Remi went to her old friend, held her, and cried. She wanted so bad to save her, but she knew there was no other way. Remi asked Colt if they could take Eris with them back to the mountains and give her a proper funeral. Colt began to understand that this journey might involve a lot of this, and he knew he needed to begin talking to the others about what comes next, after they die. He figured now that they had everybody for the journey, it would be a suitable time to start training them physically and spiritually.

"Remi, I saw a perfect spot as we were coming through the mountains close to the river that would be perfect for her final resting spot. Plus, I think it would be a good place for us to start training, I mean yes, we won against Eris but from what you say she is nothing compared to Ragnar, and we barely beat her." stated Colt.

The team filled Emmalyn and Lyndsey in on everything about being the chosen ones and fighting to save the world, which seemed like nothing new after what they just experienced. Emmalyn pulled Remi away from the group and asked her if she knew of a way to get their families back. It would be hard to leave home knowing it had been wiped off the map and there wasn't anyone left to rebuild it and make it a home worth coming back to.

"I believe she used the hurricane to trap them in another dimension, allowing her to draw her magic and power from them. I believe with your help and the sword; we can bring them back." Remi said with a soft smile.

Together Remi, Emmalyn, and Lyndsey held the Sword of Chaos and summoned the hurricane that destroyed Scarbury. It brought back everyone it took from them, a little battered and bruised but overall, they were ok.

Emmalyn and Lyndsey found their families and hugged them tight but explained what had happened and what they needed to do now. Their families understood, after what they just went through, and so they helped them pack and meet with everyone that their girls would be traveling with and cook them one last home cooked meal before they headed off into unknown territory. Colt and Lyndsey's dad built a bon-fire, and everyone gathered around for the night, one last night as kids, one last night of fun, one last night before they marched off to war.

Colt asked everyone to gather around the fire as he bowed his head and began to pray, "Lord, we don't know what tomorrow brings, but we know you lead us and protect us. God keep us safe on our journey and let us do what we need to as peacemakers for you like it says in Matthew 5:9. Guide us and bring us back home safe. We love you Lord, In your name, Amen."

The next morning, they loaded up and said goodbye, and drove away, this time not looking for a sword, but to go train and get ready to fight a monster. They headed back towards the mountains and to the opening Colt saw before when they passed through.

Chapter 7
Mountain Training

Along the banks of the Bluff River there was a beautiful clearing that sat tucked inside the edge of a mountain. It had protection on three sides and a small opening on the fourth making it a very safe place to stay for a while and train. Colt had noticed an old farmhouse before, but it looked like no one had been here in many years. They searched the area looking for anyone who might live here but found no traces of anyone living here. Between the house and the barn there was enough room for everyone and every creature to find a place to sleep and eat. They would call this place home for the next few months while they learn more about their swords and each other. Colt and Remi found a nice spot up on a ridge that overlooked the peaceful farm and flowing fields of wheat left unattended, waiting to be harvested.

Colt and Remi kept everyone on a strict schedule. Everyday wake up was at 5:30 a.m., breakfast was done by 7 and training began by 8 and they always ended the day with a bible study around a fire while having dinner. So far, everyone has pulled Colt aside at some point and asked how to get saved. He has prayed with many of them and discussed what it means to be saved and how to ask Jesus into their hearts. They also had a night where they went down to the river and Colt got to Baptize them. There are still a few that have questions and aren't quite sure what they believe yet, so Colt just continues to answer their questions and show them the love and guidance they need from a father-like figure.

Remi spends everyday teaching a different pair about their sword. Her job is to help them unlock and master all the power within the sword and themselves. They had to know exactly how they connect with their sword and how to let that power flow freely through them.

As the weeks went on and the training grew more intense, so did the questions about their faith. Colt noticed they were beginning to discuss it amongst themselves and walk each other through tough questions without Colt having to be a part of it. They have become disciples to each other and are beginning to reach the others that have been skeptical. Colt was immensely proud to see these kids were growing and maturing. He looked at this group of kids as his own now, they were in his care, and they were fighting side by side with his own daughter.

After a few months of training, Remi decided they were ready for battle. Colt learned to fight with Ranger, Dallas mastered the Sword of Fire while Kane learned to fight with Thraxal, and everyone else took turns learning their sword just in case one falls the other would be ready to take up their sword and continue fighting.

Unfortunately, on the last day of their training Emma took a hard blow to the head from Kay while using the Sword of Power. Colt rushed her into the farmhouse and for the next few days it was very touch and go. They weren't sure if she would pull through, but for now she was laying there in a coma. Eliza never left her side, in fact she barely even ate or slept. Until she woke up, there was no way they could leave the farm and hunt down Ragnar, but Colt began to send out pairs as scouts.

They would come back with nothing. Occasionally they would find some supplies or hear some stories about where Ragnar might be. On one scouting mission though, A.B. and Kay, decided to go further than usual and pushed on until they came to a forest that seemed to go on forever. The only thing that stopped it out in the distance looked like a massive castle that had been swallowed up by the forest. They knew they couldn't make it there and back before the others began to worry, so they turned around and headed back to the farm. They noticed someone in the distance was watching them but then just like that, they disappeared.

"We need to move fast and keep an eye out for anyone following us," A.B. said cautiously, "I think we are being followed and I don't want to lead them back to the others."

They took every back road they could think of and every few hours they would duck into a building or behind some rocks and wait for an hour. Surely if anyone was following them, they would get tired of their games and either give up or come try to find them. It took the girls a lot longer to get home than they planned and after a few days they knew the others would be worried. They decided no one was following them at this point and took the quickest route back to the farm, where they found everybody gathering up the supplies and getting ready to come looking for them, even Emma. She finally came out of her coma, she was still weak, but ready to move.

The girls told them about being followed and about the castle they found. They decided that it might have an armory and have shields and helmets for everyone. They figured it was worth exploring to find out, at the very least it might be a good place to make a stand against Ragnar if they need somewhere to fall back to.

It was settled they would follow A.B. and Kay and go find the Monkey Kingdom, well that's what Klaus started calling it at least. Everyone was on edge though knowing someone might be watching them, someone connected to Ragnar. Could he really know where they are and have spies following them? They moved quickly, watching everywhere, making sure no one was following them. Again, A.B. noticed someone off in the distance watching them, hiding behind trees, and following behind them as they got close to the forest edge. As the group moved on A.B. let her dad know and she hid in the bushes along the road without being seen. The rest continued moving to keep the mystery person following them, so A.B. could catch them off guard.

As the girl got closer A.B. noticed she wasn't quite human, in fact she looked a lot like the trees around her. It was a Dryad or a tree fairy, and this must be her forest. A.B. remembers learning in school that you must get their permission to enter their forest or the Dryad's can become very mean and we were about to cross into her forest, she had to stop everyone.

A.B. jumped out in front of the Dryad which alerted the others. She then bowed before her and asked her for permission to enter the forest. She told her tale of why they needed to enter and what they were looking for and then waited for the Dryad to answer.

"My name is Zada, and this is my forest and all within it belongs to me. The castle in which you speak is mine, but I will let you use it if you are worthy. Only two of you know what it is to lose everything and think all is lost only to find it again and then to selflessly give it all up again to go save people they don't even know. You, Emmalyn, and you, Lyndsey, are worthy and can take your friends into my forest. You may take whatever you need from my castle, just leave my trees and plants alone. Many who travel through here will cut down my trees for fire or pick my flowers just to smell them and then throw them away." Reeya told the group.

Zada pointed them down the right path and told them to follow the crimson flowers along the pathway and as she said it, a trail of dark crimson, blood colored, flowers began popping up in a line down the pathway. They thanked her and began on their journey into the forest.

Chapter 8
Under Cover of Forest

Zada has been the guardian of the Pickton Forest ever since she ran off a horrible King that was set on destroying her forest...her home. She couldn't stand by any longer and one day she lost control and let her anger take over and she wiped out half of the king's guard. The King ran and told others the forest was haunted, and no one was ever to go back there and left his kingdom to be overrun by the trees and plants.

No one had stepped foot into the fortress since it had been abandoned. Everything had been left behind because they left in such a hurry.

Many have wandered into Zada's woods, but few have ever made back out. She watches over her forest very carefully, making sure no one ever mistreats it like the king did. She hopes that one day someone will come along that will care as much for her plants as she does.

Being a tree spirit, she can be in many separate places and use the trees to see what is happening in various parts of the forest. Zada noticed a new face close to her forest and as soon as she began to watch her, she left. There was something about her that seemed different, and she hoped to get a chance to see her again.

Days went by and Zada began to wonder if the girl was gone forever, when suddenly, she saw her again, this time with a much larger group of people. Zada didn't trust large groups like this and so she followed at a distance to see what they were here doing. She looked away for a second and when she looked back, the girl wasn't with the group anymore. She moved cautiously closer to the group when the girl jumped out in front of her, causing her to stumble back on the ground. Just as she was about to lash out on the group, Emmalyn came over and helped her up, which caught her off guard. She wasn't used to people being nice to her, they usually tried to take something from her or destroy her forest. Zada decided this girl might be the one she would allow into her forest and even into her kingdom.

As they told her their story and asked to enter the castle, Zada knew she had plenty of supplies for the group and she wanted to help Emmalyn and her friends. She showed them the way to her castle and told them they could take whatever they needed for their journey.

As the group got closer to the castle, they realized just how massive this fortress really was. The walls stood high above the treetops and as they looked around, they couldn't see an end to the wall in either direction. It took all the Protectors to open the massive gate which was overgrown with vines. As they entered the main hall, they looked around in amazement, the inside of this castle was so well preserved.

Chapter 9
Rockdale Stronghold

Everything still looked the way it did the day the King fled. As they explored throughout the castle, Colt found the armory which was filled with shields and armor and everything they needed to prepare for battle. In the middle of what Colt is now calling their war room, was a large table with five sides. He figured there was enough room for everyone to sit around the table, but he imagined the five swords on the table pointing towards the middle, much like the knights of the round table. The more Colt looked around, the more he wanted to use this fortress as they battled Ragnar. He knew he would have to talk to Zada first, but this would be their best chance of survival and defense.

The group joined Colt in the armory and began to try on helmets and chain metal. They passed shields around to see which one fitted better to each person. A.B. walked out with a full suit of armor on, it was all black with red trim pieces. It looked like it was made for her, and she looked ready for battle. Klaus on the other hand came out with mix matched armor and some parts seemed tight, while others seemed to want to fall off. A.J. swapped out a few pieces of armor with Klaus and they finally had their armor ready to go. Everyone came out one by one with similar armor and helped check everything was on correctly, but then out came Emmalyn, wearing what must have been the Queens armor. It was made of gold and clearly hand forged and much lighter than everyone else's. Colt decided he would use the King's armor, since it was the only armor that would fit him. He was much larger than the rest of the group as was the King's armor, and it came with a nice battle axe. Colt even used spare pieces of armor to make some armor for Ranger.

As the group took their spots around the table and began discussing what would happen next, Zada came in to check on them, to see if they found what they needed.

"Thank you for everything, this is more than we could have ever asked for, but I fear I have to ask for just a little more. We need a strong and safe place to fight from against Ragnar, and this castle has everything we need. Is there any way we can bring the fight here and make this our stronghold?" pleaded Colt.

After thinking for a few minutes, Zada began speaking, "You all have treated me with kindness and respect, which I am so thankful for. I believe you are the chosen ones that will save our world and if there is anything I can do to help with that, then I am in. If you can draw his army into my woods, I can help take out many of his army, making it a much more even fight. I will also show you the tunnels that lead out from the castle, that will allow you to move around undetected, and allow you to attack from all sides."

Zada agreed to help them set up defenses around the castle and throughout the woods. They knew that once they left the castle, the next time they would be coming back, they would be coming with an army on their tails.

Zada was watching the forest edge for any signs of Ragnar or his army, they would need to know where to go soon to find him and come up with a way to get him to chase after them. They took the next week setting up traps and getting everything ready. They would always meet in the War Room at the end of the day, Colt told them the room had two purposes. One purpose was obvious: prepare for a physical battle and plan on how to win the war, and they have gone over every scenario they can think of... they are ready on this front. The other is to meet and prepare spiritually for war. They know that this will not be easy, this war will take prayer and guidance from God. They will be out manned and out matched but God has proven repeatedly, it doesn't matter the size of your army, as long as God is on your side. They spent more time in the war room in prayer as they got close to time to march towards Ragnar.

Zada, picked up one of Ragnar's spies lurking around the edge of her forest a few days ago and followed him back to Ragnar's camp. This was it; they knew it was time to move and to get their plans in motion. They would only send a few out to get his attention. They didn't want to risk everyone getting caught or worse.

Chapter 10
Ragnar Hunting

Colt led four kids, along with two protectors to go hunt down Ragnar. They knew a general area he would be in, but they knew he would never stay in one place for long. Colt knew they would have to be careful, but they would have to get as close as they could to get Ragnar's attention, they would need him to see a few of their swords.

Zada told Colt it would take them close to six days to get to the area Ragnar was last seen in. That gives Ragnar six days to move around and find a new place to hide.

Colt took to the skies on Ranger, allowing him to see ahead of their convoy for any dangers that might be ahead. Eliza and Dallas followed on Thraxal, Klaus and Lyndsey followed in Colt's truck with Alioth and Neferes. The seven began their trip to hunt down Ragnar, as they headed north through the forest, Zada showed them the quickest path out. They knew if they were in the forest, they were safe and their path was clear, making their first few days of traveling easy. Once they reached the edge of the forest though, they knew they would draw attention and if they weren't careful Ragnar could find them before they could find him.

As the group approached the forest edge, they thanked Zada for helping them and decided to make camp inside the tree line, this would be their last chance to rest safely. Colt and Dallas took the first watch while the others slept for a few hours. In the distance, just as the sun hid behind the horizon, Colt noticed what looked like hundreds of fireflies flickering on a summer night. As he looked closer, he realized that it was hundreds of campfires, it had to be Ragnar's army. He didn't realize how large his army would be, but he began to realize that tomorrow they would have thousands chasing them and there would be no room for error.

"God, we are vastly outnumbered, and we need your hand to protect us. Tomorrow we will come face to face with our enemy. I feel like David standing before Goliath, I ask you Lord to give me the same courage to stand in your name. I'm leading these kids into a situation where no kid should ever be, but it is the way it must be. Please protect them and give them the strength they need. Amen." prayed Colt.

The next morning everyone discussed the plans to draw out Ragnar. Colt took Eliza and her Sword of Sight and began moving straight for Ragnar. Dallas took Lyndsey and the Sword of Fire and circled around to the left and began their approach. Finally, Klaus took his Sword of Speed and the protectors and moved in from the right. The plan was to draw out a small group to see what Colt and Eliza were doing and then flank them from both sides, cutting them off from Ragnar. Hopefully by capturing his soldiers, allowing them to see the swords, and then releasing them, they would take the news to Ragnar himself. Once they released their captives they turned and began retreating to the woods. As Eliza looked back, she saw a man much larger than the others, barking orders at everyone. It must be Ragnar, it worked, he was mad, and he wanted their swords. As he let out a battle cry, Ragnar's army began advancing slowly at first and then it became a sprint. It seemed like a competition to see who could reach them first.

They made their way back to the tree line as arrows zoomed past them. His army was right behind them now, they would need the woods to help slow them down but remain within sight. Colt began hearing traps snapping and the enemy wailing. He knew it would help but it wasn't going to be enough, there were too many after them, he knew when he reached the clearing ahead, he would have to send up the signal to the others to come join them.

The moment they were in the clearing Thraxal shot a fire ball into the air for the others to see. The castle wasn't far away but there was no way they would make it before being overrun. A.B. spotted the fireball and everyone gathered their weapons and moved towards the clearing.

As Colt and the other's prepared to defend their ground they turned and noticed Ragnar's army had stopped before coming into the clearing. As the others joined them, they decided if they moved fast, they knew they could make it back to the fortress.

As the group got to the gates of the castle Emmalyn looked back and realized no one was following them. In fact, Ragnar's army was still on the other side of the clearing.

"Why are they not coming after us?," questioned Emma.

"I don't know, but it seems this battle won't happen like we wanted. We can use the castle as a place to fall back to, but it would seem, we will have to fight out in the open." Colt said solemnly.

They gathered their weapons and quickly discussed how they trained. They suited up and quickly gathered to pray one last time before marching into the path of their enemy.

Colt began to pray as everyone circled around, "Lord, send down your angels to protect us. Lead us against the evil that stands before us. When we can't stand any longer push us just a bit farther. If any of us shall fall today, then we will enter your kingdom with honor. Help us face our giants and stand victorious. In your name Lord amen."

Chapter 11
Heroes are Made

Alioth and Aetos stood at the gates as the others prepared to march towards the battlefield. The two protectors pushed open the gates and marched on opposite sides of the formation. Alioth turned into his tiger form and began to lead the charge, followed by Neferes as she turned into her mustang form. Slowly they all began to charge directly towards Ragnar. Colt flew left on Ranger, followed by Eliza and Emma. As the group made it to the tree line, they understood why Ragnar had not met them on the open field. Ragnar's army was hiding in the woods, and it was much larger than they had realized, but it was too late to turn back.

As the battle began Kane and Thraxel flew low and blew a fire line to cut off a huge part of Ragnars army. Colt flew high above the tree line to get a better view of how large Ragnars army was.

Colt murmured to himself, "There must be 10,000 warriors. God, please send us help, we are outnumbered!"

As Colt rejoined the group in battle, they were quickly pushed back out of the woods. In fact, they were pushed halfway across the field. Ragnar's warriors fell back to the wood line and worked to put out the fire line to free the rest of the army.

Ragnar blew his horn signaling to his entire army it was time to decimate this little group, that was just merely an annoyance to him.

As they began to march out from the tree line, a heavy fog rolled in across the field, blocking Ragnar's view of Colt's fighters.

"Guy's, we need to take advantage of this fog. I say we strike fast and retreat into the fog. If we continue to do this, from all different sides, they won't know where to attack. I think we can take a good chunk out before the fog lifts." Colt said as he motivated his worn and tired soldiers. As he looked at them, he was sad to think what he was asking them to do.

"God is in control! He has us covered, covered by fog. He will be with us through the end!" exclaimed A.B. and everyone screamed and cheered with their most fierce battle cries.

Colt loved to hear them cheering "God is in control," but he wondered if Ragnar could hear them. He figured he was laughing at their cries compared to his army.

As Colt led his warriors out of the fog to make their first attack, they stopped just outside of the fog. They never expected to see this. No one spoke for what seemed like an eternity.

As Colt watched, Ragnar's army began to take a knee and drop their weapons. Ragnar was furious and began to take out his own soldiers around him. Colt could not understand what was happening, they were surrendering. A.B stepped forward to get a better look. As she turned to ask her dad what was happening, she saw the answer to her question. As she looked at her friends standing in front of the fog, she also saw the silhouette of a mighty army in the fog. In fact, it looked like an army of angels, too large to count. They looked like giants standing at least 3 feet taller than any of her friends.

"Guys, God has our backs, look behind you" shouted A.B.

As the group began to shout again, so did the warriors standing behind them and it sounded like a mighty lion roaring and ready to charge.

Ragnar's army began to flee and after a few minutes all that stood before them was Ragnar. As he realized he was on his own, he dropped his weapon. Dallas cautiously approached with Klaos right behind him. Dallas grabbed Ragnar's sword and Klaos grabbed his battle axe, as Dallas lifted the sword Ragnar grunted, "go ahead and just finish me off!"

"I am a child of God. I'm not here to needlessly take a life. "Dallas exclaimed proudly.

Remi stepped forward and looked Ragnar in the eyes. She then realized what she would have to do. All this time she has been protecting these swords and believed they were the only way to save the world, but now she realizes everything Colt has told her about God is true. She knows these swords do hold a lot of power and they can't be left for anyone to use for evil, so she decides to destroy them. As she looks around, she realizes this group of unknown heroes are only heroes because they truly and wholeheartedly trusted in God.

Ragnar was sentenced to life in the castle dungeon. Remi lets him out to guard the castle though and has begun telling him about God. As for the rest of our heroes they still have a long journey home.

Chapter 12
Journey's End

"I can't believe it has been almost a year ago when I first saw you, Remi, standing in my room, scaring the bejesus out of me." laughed A.B.

"You have grown so much since then, I am so proud to call you my friend, more like a sister really. I will miss all of you so much. Please come see me sometimes." replied Remi.

"I do believe we might come down here on this day, every year, to remember our victory given to us by God. I personally never want to forget that all things are possible through Jesus. My God is bigger, stronger, braver, and can never be defeated." shouted Colt as he walked through the group as they hugged Remi and said their goodbyes.

As they packed up their stuff and began their journey home, Colt knew it would be a long journey home and there was still a chance of running into small groups of Ragnar's soldiers along the way. They would be ready. This group of kids...well they really didn't seem like kids anymore, they had grown up right in front of his eyes, and they can take on anything because they had God on their side.

As the group moved down the path, they decided to follow the same route they took getting here. As they passed through the mountains they stopped at Eris's grave, paid their respects, and left flowers from Remi. Then just as they joined the group, one pair at a time left the group as they passed through their hometowns.

Colt met with everyone's families as they dropped them off and told their tales from the last year and how they were heroes. They were simply happy to have their kids back and thanked Colt for keeping them safe.

It took them several months to take everyone home and finally to come back to Elberta. A.B.'s mom spotted them coming down the road and began to run to welcome them home. Annabeth couldn't stop telling her mom everything that had happened over the last year. In fact, she talked so much, and she was so tired from traveling, she fell asleep in the middle of telling her mom about her new sister, Remi.

Colt took Annabeth to her room and put her in her bed.

"Goodnight, I'm so proud of you" whispered Colt, as he closed her door.

A bright light woke Annabeth from a deep sleep. It was Remi again, this time she didn't scare Annabeth. In fact, Annabeth wanted to go get her mom and introduce them, but Remi stopped her.

"Annabeth, you are all in danger. Ragnar's brother is looking for him. He has heard from some of his soldiers about you all. He is looking for you." Remi said solemnly.

"It's ok, we will be ready. This time we will have our families join us. We will train them, and we will have God marching with us." exclaimed A.B.

Word was sent out to everyone explaining what was coming and they were told to meet up on what they now call Mount Eris with their families. As they gathered, they knew they could face anything if they stand together and stand for God.